I0623755

THE GOTH & THE HOUSEWIFE

MAFIA, MURDER, AND MAYHEM SERIES (AS A
NOVELETTE)

ELM JED

ELM JED
Author - Creator

Paperback ISBN - 9781967019175

Ebook ISBN - 9781967019168

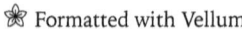 Formatted with Vellum

CONTENT WARNINGS

Content Warnings

On page:
Restraining orders & stalking, chasing (not the fun kind),
slight blood and gore, guns, knives, physical fights, name
calling, coercion, and death.

Discussed in this story:
Domestic & physical abuse, including suggestion of sexual
abuse

To those who thought they couldn't start over,
yes you can.
It's never too late to leave the closet.

BOOK PLAYLIST

"Which Witch" - Florence + The Machine
"Fangtasy" - Bambie Thug
"Touch" - I, Us, & We
"Call the Ships to Port"- Covenant
"mary magdalene" - FKA Twigs
"Beloved" - VNV Nation
"Shout Out to My Ex" - Little Mix
"Mary On A Cross" - Ghost
"Passenger" - Deftones
"Paint it Black" - Hidden Citizens, Rånya
"Toxic" - 2WEI
"Slowlove" - BLACKBOOK
"Pink Pony Club" - Chappell Roan
"I Love Lucy Theme Song"

CHAPTER 1
JESSE HATES LUCY

I SHOULD'VE POISONED THE POT ROAST.

My thoughts ramble as I press myself against the wall opposite of the door to my small apartment. It's a studio, bedroom, living room, and kitchen rolled into one, so the only true separate space was the bathroom. Bookshelves are everywhere due to a librarian living here before. A comfortable and quaint space if my abusive ex-husband wasn't pounding on the door.

I run my hands nervously over my floral print tea dress, staying silent in hopes he'll go away.

How did Jesse find me?

"I know you're in there, Lucy!" That baritone voice rattles me, making me touch the cheek he slapped long ago.

I can almost remember a time when those blue eyes were charming. Back when I was naïve and wouldn't realize until years later it was all a rouse. Fake. Fifteen years of marriage, down the drain. In a few months I'll be thirty-six, only recently beginning to feel actual freedom.

He pounds the door again and I clench my jaw. I glance

at my knives, wondering if I had the strength to fight him off again.

I moved out of Connecticut to New York City a few months ago, then got a job at a Paranormal owned company where my boss is an incubus. My desk buddy, Rhonda, is a pale, brown werewolf who's the nicest being I've met. We've traded recipes. My neighborhood was also mostly Paranormal beings. Every day here made me wish I'd grown up around them more than humans, especially the last ten years. My divorce lawyer is also a werewolf, who's tried to push Jesse's lawyers to sign the damn paperwork.

He hasn't. And he shouldn't know where I live. Must have illegally obtained my address even though I have a restraining order against him.

The door bangs again.

I lean my head back, unsure of what to do. I could call my lawyer? What could he do though? Jesse's already ignoring the divorce papers and restraining order.

Finally, the knocking stops when I hear my neighbor yelling at him. It's early afternoon on a Saturday, sleeping hours for most Paranormals, even if they live on Topside. I breathe easier when footsteps move away. Quietly, I go to the door and look out the peep hole. He's gone.

I quickly grab my cardigan and purse, holding them close as I go open the door. I wince from the lingering pain in my shoulder and ache within my wrist from Jesse. Our most recent fight when he caught me outside the courthouse... until my lawyer showed up, thankfully.

I slowly open the door.

"You, okay?"

I yelp, jumping as I clutch the actual pearls around my neck.

"Whoa, it's alright," says my neighbor, Riley. He's an incubus with dark maroon skin and long black hair. It's mussed somewhat hiding his small horns. He holds his hands up, making his baggy shirt rustle around him. In an instant, I calm as his powers flicker down the hall. Likely why Jesse left without a fight.

Riley and other incubi or succubi rarely use their pheromone controlling powers on just anybody. But, now it's helpful. I breathe in the warm scent of vanilla.

"That's the ex, isn't?"

"Yes, and he shouldn't know where I live," I huff. "I'm sorry—"

"Don't apologize for that asshole." He crosses his arms. "You filed that restraining order, right?" I tentatively nod, and he sighs, "Yeah, he's not gonna listen."

My chin quivers, looking down the hall.

"I think…I may go look for another apartment," I whisper, clutching my sweater. "Could I move to the Underground if I get special permissions? I don't think he'll ever go down there."

Riley stares at me, then blows out a breath. "You need to be associated with a Paranormal being, family or partner, otherwise you'd have to come back to Topside in like a month."

Maybe Rhonda will turn me into a werewolf.

Who am I kidding, I can't afford that kind of permit.

My face falls, wondering what I can do. Suddenly, Riley gestures for me to stay put and disappears into his apartment. I keep my keys sticking out between my fingers, anxiously looking down the hall. My heart clatters in my chest until he comes back and hands me a business card.

"Go here for help."

I stare at the gold embossed card. *Unbound*. A strip club. "What?"

"Owner is well-known," he answers. "He…specializes in helping beings, Paranormals and humans." I stare at him.

"Ask for Alanzo, and tell'em baby sis' old neighbor sent you."

I stare down at the card. I've no idea who this could be, but I'll take any help at this point. I was *almost* free, and maybe this was my ticket. A wave of that sweet scent hits me, and my shoulders unclench as I realize how harshly I was holding my keys.

"Thank you," I sigh.

"Welcome."

"This place...it's down in the Underground?"

"Yeah, take the Main Entrance few blocks away. It's not far."

"Won't they be sleeping?"

"Still a strip club." He smiles. "Doors are always open."

I take a deep breath, steeling myself to go to a strip club for the first time in my life and get help from some...one. Owner. Totally. Sure.

I should've poisoned that damn pot roast.

CHAPTER 2
LUCILLE GOES TO A STRIP CLUB

It's bright on Topside as I make it to the Main Entrance to the Underground of New York City. A few Paranormals walk out of the elevator, mostly shifters who quickly change into their human forms. Their once pastel colored skin and long white hair disappear as they shift. As I get on the elevator alone, I pull my cardigan closer. I've gone down to the Underground a couple times with Rhonda, who showed me her favorite tavern.

In the reflective glass of the elevator, I glance over myself. My shoulder length blond hair is curled to perfection as I always like it, matching my pale skin from rarely seeing the sun. Brown eyes stare back at me. Jesse made wear blue contacts because he said it was *prettier*.

"Asshole," I grumble.

I smooth down my dress while gazing out at the Underground as I descend. The city is built beneath NYC, mainly for Paranormals, but anyone can visit. After years of hearing about it, it was amazing to finally see. Artificial lights mimic stars and the sun; an ambiance of soft violets and blues that flicker with softer hues. Maybe, just maybe this Alanzo can help me move down here.

I arrive at the bottom, stepping out and follow Riley's directions. Walking down the mostly cobblestone path, I keep checking over my shoulder to see if Jesse is following me.

"He wouldn't be caught dead down here," I huff to myself. For years he told me the Undergrounds were too dreary, made for "monsters". In reality, the real monster was him.

His list of red flags was longer than my monthly grocery list.

I may kick myself forever for not noticing sooner.

As I get closer to *Unbound*, my heart thunders in my chest. I brace myself as I pass a closed coffee shop, and soon see the glowing neon sign of the strip club.

First step done. Found it. Good job, Lucille.

I approach who I presume is a bouncer for the club. There several other beings out front, including humans as they chatter and laugh. My spine goes rigid as a handful of men pass. I stop, fear gripping me.

I've never been in a strip club or *any* club. I'd been a housewife for 15 years for fuck sakes.

Jesse told me how seedy they were, and it wasn't a place for me. Yet, he went all the damn time. I glance at my attire, feeling like a fish out of water. Bemoaning inside myself, I wonder again if I can do this. Nerves getting to me, I turn away about to give up, but then stop myself.

"No. You are walking in there, Lucille," I tell myself. "You love floral. You love dresses, even if Jesse hated them, doesn't mean those inside will. Strip club or not. So..." I stand straighter, and turn on my heel, "...walk in there."

The bouncer, an incubus with bright blue eyes and

leathery wings looming over him, smiles as I approach. "New here?"

I clear my throat. "Yes, I am."

He smiles broader, then pulls out a clipboard and starts reviewing the rules of the club. "No touching workers, dancers, or strippers without permission. They're not allowed to touch you without permission. If the pheromones overwhelm you, tell an employee. Backrooms are for incubi and succubi only; special permissions can be granted, but you have to speak with one of the owners. No belligerent behavior or language. No overly drunkenness. No drugs. If you notice someone being unsafe, report them. Turnover for brunch is at dusk, but the club will remain open."

"You have brunch?"

"Yup." He winks, handing me the pen and paper. "This waiver is good for six months before you need to sign another, it also includes you agreeing to what I just said."

"Ah, okay...and thank you, sir." I sign my name.

"Name's Darius. Call if you need anything, but relax and enjoy the shows."

Releasing a breath, I step into the club and am almost overcome by a world I've never experienced. Everything is violet and crimson, deep hues lit by low lights, and a few directed at stages. It smells wonderful, filled with warmth and spices. It's sensually soothing as I walk further in and see velvet walls and plush furniture. Every stage has a pole, and the biggest stage has three with strippers performing.

My eyes widen as I watch for a moment, something blooming at my core that makes my skin feel flush. Blushing, I turn away and make my way to the bar. There's an incubus bartender with a light scarlet skin tone mixing drinks. The human men I saw before grab their drinks, walking away to their seats to watch a stripper on a smaller stage.

"What can I get you?" I jump at the question, turning back to the bartender who grins softly. "Easy, first timer. You're safe here."

"Apologies. Can you really tell it's my first time?"

"A bit. Drink to help?" He asks sweetly. Tingling occurs over me, and my nerves lessen as I breathe deep.

A drink sounds perfect after today. Maybe some liquid courage to help.

"What do you recommend?"

"Any cocktail I make."

"And if I've never had anything other than wine before?"

"Do you want wine?"

"Oh, goodness no, I hate it." I clear my throat at my reaction. His smile softens, then holds up a finger.

"I think I have something for you," he says, beginning to mix a drink. He finishes, placing a pink colored drink in front of me. "Called Sweet Paradise. First drink is on me."

"Thank you." I take it, sipping the cocktail and my eyes widen. It's delicious. He must notice I like it because he winks and starts to walk away. "Actually...I'm looking for someone."

"Dancer perhaps?" He asks, coming back over.

"Someone named Alanzo?" His pale blue eyes flick over me, assessing suddenly. What else did Riley say to do? "Baby sis' old neighbor sent me."

Surprise moves over him. "Oh, uh I can deliver a message for him. He's not gonna be available until brunch starts."

"I can wait."

What would that message even be? *Help a human move to the Underground? Get rid of my ex-husband.* Oh, I wish.

He nods, leaving to clean glasses. I take my cocktail and find an empty couch. The club isn't packed with people, but finding a small piece to myself helps. Different dancers are on stage as music plays, helping drown out my thoughts. I sip my drink, enjoying the sweet taste and wondering if I can get the recipe. It's awhile before I finish, and a waitress comes by to grab the empty glass and asks if I want another. I get an iced tea instead.

As the minutes tick by, I wonder if I should truly wait. I could go to the large library down here. Maybe explore the Underground more. Except, I still worry Jesse may have followed me down here. I doubt he'd make it into *Unbound*, but still the fear lingers. I smooth my dress out.

Determined to wait, I settle into my seat once more.

Two second later, I mumble to myself, "What am I doing? How is talking to this Alanzo going to—"

Suddenly the lights shift, darkening the stages. The announcer introduces, "Welcome to the stage…Dany!"

The spotlight goes to the main stage not far from me. Out walks a succubus with rouge skin, tattooed with white and black ink. The sides of her head are shaved, wavy black hair stopping at the nape of her neck. She wears a leather vest and thong, long fingerless gloves to her elbows, and platform boots that lace up past her knees. My breath catches as my eyes are unable to tear away from her thick thighs covered in ripped mesh stockings. Hard beats of music start as she dances, gliding around the pole as if she's not wearing those enormous boots.

They *have* to be heavy.

I'm entranced by her. Her vest is torn off, revealing spiked pasties upon her nipples. I blush, my throat going dry as I forget about anything outside this club. Her breasts are bigger than mine and they bounce as she dances, spinning on the pole. She lands upon her knees, slamming her fists down as shouts erupt through the club. The succubus crawls seductively over the stage in *my* direction.

My eyes widen. She's maybe twelve feet from me, too far and yet too close. Cobalt eyes find mine, searing into me as her pierced tongue runs over her teeth.

Oh. Fuck. Me.

CHAPTER 3
VACATION FROM DIVORCE

I DON'T THINK I'M STRAIGHT.

The succubus, Dany, keeps dancing on stage for another song. I stare after her as she gyrates on the stage, lifting her hips. What would that tongue piercing feel like if she kissed—

Calm down, Lucille.

You're here to find someone to help you. But not like that. Well, maybe…NO.

The music ends, and the announcer introduces someone else. I don't dare look up from my iced tea, afraid of the amount of blushing I'll do if I see her again. Sipping my drink, I try to be calm and tell myself it's just because I'm in this club. That's all. I'm stressed after Jesse tried to break in. Not because I haven't been properly fucked in…my entire life.

Oh, that's depressing. Maybe I do need another cocktail.

"Hello there, darling." A sultry voice startles me.

I almost drop my drink onto the table, looking up at the stripper I'd been rethinking my entire life over. She smiles, tilting her head. Closer, I see she has a septum piercing that's onyx, matching the piercings on her brow and ears. My eyes try not to move down to her breasts, naked aside from the pasties.

What else is pierced?

I squeak, "Hello."

"Mind if I sit?"

A nod is all I can give. She sits right beside me with her thigh brushing mine. Heat blossoms inside me, traveling up my chest.

"Name's Dany. You?"

"Lucille."

"Beautiful name," she comments, leaning back into the sofa. I try not to stare at her breasts, truly wondering if her nipples are also pierced.

When have I ever cared about that? About five minutes ago, when I wanted to lick—

"I love your dress," Dany says, bringing her arm around to lay over the back of the sofa, careful to not touch me. "The floral pastels suit you."

Surprised, I meet her gaze. "Are you just saying that because it's your job?"

She chuckles deep, sighing a bit after. "No, honeybun. In this line of work, I certainly don't need to give empty compliments to get tips."

I blanch a little. "I'm sorry. This is my first time...well, this is my first time."

Dany tilts her head, assessing me before she swings a leg over her other. A part of me wants to stare at her thighs or perhaps touch the shiny leather going up her shin.

"This place is different than most anyways," she says, not seeming offended.

I hum as I run my hands over my skirt.

"Are those hard to walk in?" I gesture to her boots, which I'm sure are almost 4-6 inches thick on the bottom.

"No harder than your heels." She nods at mine. "You practice in yours; I practice in mine." She leans in closer. "It's also goth magic."

A giggle escapes me. I become less rigid as I smell a rich perfume. Her eyes meet mine, and for a moment I truly do forget about my troubles. What I'm running from.

"How do you feel about touch, honeybun?"

I'm not sure why she keeps calling me that, but I don't want her to stop.

"Yeah...uh...it's okay," I whisper timidly.

She glides her hand over my skirt, and my thigh feels like it becomes alight. Her fingers adorned with rings brush the fabric, humming to herself as I stare at her. My breaths are shallow as the music thumps in the club. Her head tilts again, watching me as if I'm as delicate as the flowers I wear.

"Really does suit you," she says as her arm on the sofa moves close, touching my back. She's warm. "Flowers and pastels."

I laugh suddenly. Her hand slides up, stopping midway on my thigh. She leans in closer, not quite invading my space, but...sharing it.

"Why does that make you laugh?"

"Didn't take you for someone who'd like flowers or... colors." I nod toward her outfit.

"I only wear dark colors, leather, jeans, but yours..." she traces one of the flowers, "...I can appreciate items that suit you. Like pastels. Flowers. Or just a gorgeous skirt."

She lifts the fabric up a little. That perfume surrounds me, and I lean further back into the couch not caring about my posture.

"They help me feel pretty," I say.

"You are with them or without." She continues to stroke

my thigh. "Why don't you tell me more about what you like, Lucille?"

"I'm not...I mean..." I huff, glancing back at the bartender and remembering why I'm here. "Maybe there's someone else you can talk to."

A finger is placed under my chin, lightly moving my head to look directly at her. Cobalt eyes glimmer warmly.

"I'm asking because I want to talk with you, honeybun." She smiles. "I'm a stripper, and I've stripped. My job's done, so why don't we relax on my off-time?"

Her touch is so gentle. A sweetness I'm not used to and a sense of safety washes over me. A shiver goes down my back. A part of me can't help hearing Jesse, telling me he's protecting me from the outside world. People who'd trick me and use me. Yet, he'd been the only one who had for years. After so long of feeling discarded, I crave the attention Dany is willing to give me. Real or not.

I had hours before I could meet with Alanzo, why not indulge this fantasy for one day to feel better? To have what Jesse took from me. I already feel more comfortable with her *not* being a man.

Placing my hand over hers, I smile and nod. She grins, but not before sweeping her tongue over her top lip. A spike of heat hits me as I swallow hard, but I talk.

For hours I converse with Dany.

Things I've always wanted to talk about, I tell her. She listened, while watching me intently. Our attention was undivided until some crowds of men arrived, and I found myself looking over my shoulder every few minutes. Dany moved us to another sofa, away from the beings filling the club. She left to change, and now I sit ramrod straight until she returns.

I sip my second cocktail. I'd relented as I felt myself become as nervous as when I arrived. It shouldn't be long until I can meet with Alanzo. Melancholy fills me of my time ending with Dany, not wanting to separate from her. That feeling dissipates when I see her coming back.

Dany changed into leather leggings, a dark bikini top with an open shiny long vest, and platform boots that now buckle up to her knees. She saunters towards me, but two men try to catch her attention. She's taller than them, an unamused look passes over her that makes them quickly step away. Nodding once at the bartender, she strides to me, and her expression becomes something sweeter.

"Miss me, honeybun?" She sinks into the cushions beside me.

I go to say yes, but close my mouth. Not wanting to seem needy, I just smile pleasantly. Chuckling low, she puts her arm around me and leans in close to whisper, "Missed you, too."

I blush, and then fidget with my skirt as my heart flutters. Every few minutes I still wonder what her tongue could do. Or fingers. I quickly brush those thoughts away, reminding myself that this can't be real. Just a one-time thing to keep busy until I find Alanzo.

Right? Right.

Her breath drifting over my jaw and cheek are not helping me keep that opinion.

"How much do you know about succubi, honeybun?" She asks suddenly, trailing a hand over my leg.

My breath hitches at the soft gesture. "Not a lot, but I've been learning. I have a neighbor who's an incubus. Oh, that sounds like...I'm—"

She hums, turning my face to look at her. "I understand what you're saying."

I exhale sharply in relief.

"I find it a tragedy how plainly you speak about your

wonderful joys, yet I know you've not experienced pure pleasure of the body."

My eyes widen. "How—?"

"Succubi and incubi like myself, who are strong enough, can sense it. Practically smell it. For you it's not a lack exactly...but how you react newly to what's around here. And to me."

Embarrassment wants to flood me as I try to turn away, from her, but Dany keeps her tender grip upon my chin.

"There's something else, darling," she continues, keeping me focused on her gemstone eyes. "Your pheromones entice me. Near you, it's as if I'm breathing in the essence of spring itself. Last rays of sun which turn the sky to glorious pinks with the sound of spring thunderstorms on the horizon. Exquisite. Perilous."

"I'm not that..."

"Trust me, honeybun, you are. I'm over a hundred years old, dancing and stripping for decades...no one's held me in such a way."

"You don't mean that."

"I do."

We're inches apart. Her eyes hooded with desire I've never seen before directed towards me. There's a seriousness in her gaze, telling me this may not be completely a game of fantasy.

"It's barely been hours," I gasp.

"Attraction is attraction, darling. It only requires a moment." My body shudders at her caress, leaning closer. I inhale that erotic perfume, which I know now is hers.

Her lips seem impossibly far. I clutch her hand upon my thigh, holding it for dear life.

"Allow me to show you a fragment of what you're doing to me, my beautiful storm." Dany's voice is low and inviting.

Uncertainty, along with fear simmer in my stomach, but as I gaze into her eyes those fears vanish. The thought that had come to me again and again when I left for a new life, comes back. *I want to live.*

I nod.

Music pulsating through the club, lights dimming, Dany kisses me. It's not like any of the other kisses I've had before. It's softer. Tender with a firmness that makes me gasp for breath. I sigh, opening for her as that pierced tongue traces my lips. The metal is odd, briefly swirling around my tongue as the heat within me brews. Arousal flashes between my thighs as I squeeze my legs together. Her hand gently holds the back of my head, helping tilt my mouth against hers. She tastes of robust wine and sweet-ened berries.

Fantasy or not, this was realer than anything I've experi-enced before.

Too soon, she pulls away and asks, "Trust me?"

"Uh-huh."

"Succubi and incubi are known for being...fast, it's just in our nature to love and cherish. We're very physical beings. So, just say stop if you need." Dany's hand upon my thigh slides down, dipping under my skirt and moving up my bare skin. I become rigid in surprise. "Do you want me to stop?"

My eyes flick to where her hand rests, hidden beneath my pastel floral skirt. I glance at the club, seeing dancers on stage and the lights directed at them. My heart pounds, in exhilaration and hesitation.

"No one will notice. I'll be sure of it." Dany lightly grips my chin to look at her. "I can help you relax, darling."

Should I jump off into the deep end? Or run? Oh, how sick I am of running.

Once more, I glance around, seeing no one paying attention to us. "Alright," I whisper.

The intoxicating perfume intensifies, engulfing me and
my body loses its rigidity. I sigh, relinquishing myself to
the feeling of relaxation and something wholly new. Dany
kisses my neck, moving her hand up my thigh.

The touch of her is invigorating, causing my body to
shudder. She comes closer to the apex of my thighs, and my
eyes widen. She pauses, raising a brow. Swallowing hard, I
nod my head. Curiosity now taking over, if her kiss was that
wonderful, what else could be?

Slowly, her fingers skim over my panties. My breath
catches, shivering, but then that calm state comes over me
as again as I take another deep breath. I become languid as
her fingers trace the hem of my underwear, which ignites a
fire inside me.

"You're delightful," she praises me, licking her tongue
up the side of my neck. She kisses my jaw, and I can't help
feeling...loved.

The music changes to a slower beat, thundering along-
side the pulse in my veins. I've never felt this way before.
It's fucking wonderful.

"Lucille." Her voice is a siren's call bringing my attention
back to her. I stare down at her lips, and she smiles before
kissing me again.

Her hand moves under my panties, slipping inside and I
gasp against her mouth. My legs squeeze together, not
trying to fight her off, but overwhelmed by the arousal that
builds. She hushes against my lips in a gentle manner,
easing my legs open.

"No one can see or smell you, just me," she reassures,
licking her tongue along my bottom lip. "You're all mine."

A finger circles around my clit. I jolt, gasping into her
mouth as she kisses me again. She teases me below with her

thumb and fingers, before inserting a finger into me. Although a small invasion, it feels like much more as she circles it inside me. I want to cry out, forget where I am, but concentrate on her kisses instead. The air is energized, sparking as she gently fucks me with her hand.

"Dany," I breathe out.

"Such a beautiful storm."

A second finger joins the first, spreading the two inside me. I pitch forward, huffing as I try to hide my face against her shoulder. She blissfully tortures me with her fingers, and I feel pleasure build from my core. The heat I'd felt before watching Dany comes back tenfold, drowning me as I try catch my breath with this new territory. It's glorious and torturous. I never want her stop.

"Almost there, honeybun...how about a little push?"

The perfume strengthens, and my body bows to her commands as I clutch at her arm. Her seductive words, combined with how delicately she handles me makes my breath stop. My body locks up as I tighten around her fingers. Dany circles my clit, pressing up and I shake against her caress. Pleasure like I've not known before, overwhelms me. Not long after, I drift after coming and lean back against the sofa.

"Holy...wow," I sigh, shuddering as her hand pulls out from under my skirt. Dany licks her fingers erotically in front of me, smiling with mirth. I stare in shock.

No one has ever...she...tasted me!

"I know that face, honeybun." She cups my jaw. "A first wasn't it? Oh, you truly haven't been worshipped, have you?"

I can only shake my head.

"You're so delicious. Want a taste?" She opens her mouth, offering her tongue that'd cleaned her fingers of me. The piercing glistens in the light.

I've *never* tasted myself before. Jesse always refused to do anything like that.

Clutching onto the pleasure she'd given me, and emboldened to at least try, I accept the offer. I tentatively lick her tongue, and then kiss her deeply. It's almost…salty. Not unpleasant. Honestly, I'd take it over Jesse's cum which always tasted funky.

I taste way better than him.

An odd anger bubbles inside me that it'd taken this long for me to feel like someone worth devouring. To feel that kind of pleasure. And lastly, to know *he* took away those opportunities, attempting to control what I liked and dared to do.

"What is it, honeybun?" Dany pulls back, stroking my cheek. "Didn't like it?"

"Oh, no, I loved it. Thank you," I press on a smile, but then frown. "I realized how much of life I've missed."

"Still young."

I snort, "I'm in my mid-thirties and divorced. Might as well be an old maid."

Dany snorts next, lounging back with a smirk. "No, not at all. Take it from a succubus who's 150 years old. You're young, even for a human. There's still life to live."

I sigh, looking away towards the dancers on stage.

"Isn't that why you came down here? To live a little more?" Dany asks.

My reasoning to be here comes crashing back. For the past few hours, I've almost forgotten my mission and who may be waiting for me on Topside. I sit up a little straighter, reminding myself this is only a fantasy, something that will vanish when I leave the club. Delightful and mind-opening as it was, this wasn't real.

"I came here to look for someone," I whisper. My hands move down my skirt, smoothing the fabric.

"Who? Don't say me. It'll stroke my ego," she muses, tilting her head as her arm lays over the back of the sofa behind me.

"Not a dancer," I say.

"Oh?"

"At least... I don't think they are." Would an owner of a club dance at their own establishment?

Dany raises her brows in question. "Who is it? Perhaps I can help."

"Alanzo." The warmth I've felt disappears. The perfume vanishes as her brows pinch together, lightly frowning. Is he someone that's hard to contact? A bad boss and Riley doesn't know? "Is something wrong?"

Her hand upon my thigh is taken away. It's like cold water has drenched me, and the last of my little dream bubble pops. I scoot away from her, repeating smoothing my skirt out as I take a shaky breath. Dany flicks her gaze to a door near the back of the club, then to me.

"Why are you waiting for Alanzo Cuorebella?"

Was that his last name?

I gulp, heart now pounding. "I need help."

"Such as?"

My hands wring together, but I press them down not wanting to seem "unladylike" or distracting as Jesse would say.

"To move, perhaps. Or just...I need his help."

Suddenly, Dany leans in and grips my chin to look at her. I gasp as she brings her face close to mine. Cobalt eyes flare, and that perfume spikes again, but spicier.

"There are few reasons why anyone comes to wait for him," she speaks low. "Mobsters, refugees from the black market, or those who need out of the state or country. Which one are you, Lucille?"

My eyes widen. "Did you just say mobsters?"

"Do you now know who he is?"

"I was told he could help me." I stare at her, new fear crawling. "Why did you say mobsters?"

"Because he was a mafia boss longer than I've been alive, and practically still *is*."

My stomach drops. Something tightens around my chest. I've been...waiting for a mafia boss?

"You didn't know," she whispers.

I shake my head, tearing away from her grip. "Of course, I didn't know!" I yell under my breath. I wouldn't have come down here to meet with a mafia boss.

What am I doing?

"He's not a bad incubus," she starts saying, but my thoughts run wild. "He's a generous boss, loving father, and devoted to his Mate of 600 years." I stare at the ground, realizing how old he may be. "But those looking for him, *especially* humans, are for specific things..." her voice lowers, trying to catch my attention, "...like those who need help running from monsters."

I need to leave. I wanted another chance to restart without Jesse pounding at my door or trying to hurt me. Someone like that, had to be unpredictable and dangerous. What would Alanzo want in exchange from *me*? I can't pay a mafia boss, and I'm certainly not brave enough to speak with him. I've hit my limit of bravery today.

I stumble up from my seat, grabbing my cardigan.

"I need to go."

"Lucille, I didn't mean to—"

"Thank you for your time, it was lovely." My voice is robotic like the dutiful housewife I once was. It grates at me. I wince, turning away as Dany stands next.

My head swims as I head for the exit, needing out and to rethink what I can do. I'm almost at the door when the bartender calls over to me. "Hey, the boss just showed up if you—"

My mind blanks as I follow where he gestures. First, I see Dany, prowling towards me with determination on her face. But then, I see an incubus near the back door. He barely looks over 40 with onyx hair that's swept back and has deep maroon skin. He starts to look towards me, and doom fills me.

Panic hitting, I spin on my heel and rush out of the doors. Darius calls out after me, and there's other sound, but I can't stop my feet as I race away from *Unbound*.

CHAPTER 4
LUCILLE IS ENAMORED BY A SUCCUBUS

I'm a naïve fool and a coward!

Groups of people pass me as I huff and stomp my way towards the Main Entrance. Halfway there, I stop and stare at the large elevator that reaches up to Topside. I smooth my hand over my flipping stomach, unsure if I should go back home, yet. It's only early evening up there.

"What if he's there? Waiting for me?" I murmur.

Someone grumbles at me, and I realize I've stopped in the middle of the path. I step aside, close to the coffee shop that's still closed. Perhaps, I could wait until they open. Hide down here in the Underground, until they throw me back onto Topside.

I sigh, arms dropping to my sides.

How bad would it be if I asked a mafia boss to get rid of Jesse? Could I live with that? My mind flashes to all the times Jesse has hurt *me*. I wrap my arms around myself.

"Let's be honest, Lucille...you do not *have* the kind of money to pay for someone to off your abusive ex-husband. Maybe I could invite him over for dinner, and then finally poison the pot roast...if he doesn't kill me before he takes that first bite."

My outward thoughts pause when I think I smell Dany's perfume. Thinking I'm imagining it, I turn and gasp when I see her. She practically stomps...saunters...sexily strides towards me. Her face is cool and collected as that long vest of hers rustles behind her. The being who grumbled at me, dodges from her path, along with a few others.

I stare at her, mesmerized. Desire floods back, attracted to the confidence she showcases. I assume she'll just pass me, keep moving. Instead, she stops a few feet from me and pops her hip out, crossing her arms over her chest. Even not being directly next to me, she still looms over me in those boots.

I look around, seeing if anyone will say anything. Beings ignore us as they go about their lives, while I slowly back up towards the wall of the closed shop.

"For a moment, I thought I'd have to fly after you," she says finally.

"What...why...why?" I shake my head. "What are you doing?"

"Making sure you don't go home alone."

I gape at her, and then quickly school my expression. "I don't need an...escort."

The last part is whispered, and she smirks while stepping closer. I step back, unsure of what she wants. I'm not scared of her, I feel safer with Dany than I ever have, especially with Jesse, but I feel confused. We're not in *Unbound* anymore. I'm not a potential customer. I left.

Dany comes closer, bringing her hand up slowly and strokes my hair back. She easily tucks it behind my ear as I swallow hard. My heart thunders in my chest as another zap of desire hits me. A shiver runs down my back.

"I didn't know who he was," I whisper, confusion

swamping me along with these other feelings I keep having around her. "I can't...I mean..."

"I reacted poorly, my apologies, honeybun," she says softly. "You don't need to tell me why or who you're running from, but I'm not letting you go home alone. You've become precious to me, and I'd hate to see an exquisite flower like yourself get hurt going home in such a worried state. Especially since I'm partially to blame."

"You're not," I say roughly. "You don't need to walk me home."

"I want to, Lucille."

"We just met, why would you care?"

Dany takes another step, her shadow falling over me. I have to lean my head back to look at her. She smiles softly.

"Oh, honeybun, none of this is because of my job, but because you entice me. Your pastel flowers. Blonde hair." She twirls some strands between her fingers. "Your smile and laughter. You're a fresh column of starlight, Lucille."

Was it real? Was the time I had with her not a fantasy, stuck within that club, but more? She caresses her thumb under my lip.

"Let me walk you home. Just to be sure you're safe," she tells me.

A sense of calm comes over me. Less fearful of what could be above.

I nod, and she begins to step back, but my hand shoots out to grasp her. My hand clutches the hem of her vest, gripping the thick material.

"It was real?" I whisper.

"Yes." I look up at her cobalt eyes. "Only being I've ever gotten off...that stage for is you, honeybun."

"And you'll...make sure I get home safe?" Her eyes darken, that perfume mirroring it as she nods her head. "Because I think I'm getting tired. Of running."

Dany crowds me and I move until my back is against the brick wall. She places both hands above my head, leaning over me while I still clutch her vest. I stare up, speechless as her eyes begin to glow. My eyes flick over her horns that peek through her hair, to the dark eyeliner I'd never wear, and piercings I'd never get.

My stomach flutters. Dany sears her gaze into me; a pillar protecting me from what's around us.

"Who are you running from, darling?" She asks in a soothing tone.

I don't want to answer. To not think about him. About who I was.

I swallow hard, dropping my sweater as I bring my other hand up to cup her jaw. I hadn't truly touched her inside the club, almost too fearful of breaking the daydream. Her skin is smooth. I pull her towards me, and Dany doesn't fight me. She melts into me like it was meant to be. I tilt my head back, leaning my chest against hers as her mouth comes to mine. Her arms remain above my shoulders, allowing me to pull her closer as she kisses me deeply. More butterflies are conjured in my stomach as I grip onto her.

Gone are my worries as we kiss. I feel alive and hopeful. I cling to her for dear life, for a sensation I've not felt before as desire jolts through me.

The piercing I'm enticed by flicks over my tongue and a moan escapes me. Her tongue plays with mine as I hear her moan next. It seems like forever before we finally peel apart. Dany brings a hand down, gently clutching my chin.

"Then run to me, honeybun." I nod a little as she kisses my cheek next. "Now, let me take you home."

I clear my throat, almost shivering from her soothing voice. "I live on Topside."

"Figured."

"It's not a short distance."

"Traveled further, darling." She steps back, bending down to grab my cardigan.

"Thank you," I murmur, taking it from her and feel myself blush. "This way, then."

Dany gives more room as I smooth my skirt down. I start walking, absentmindedly touching my lips, because it feels like they're buzzing. I glance over my shoulder at the apparent shadow I've gained. Dany's quiet as she follows me closely like a Valkyrie ready to strike.

My thoughts become fuzzy, wondering why I even made out with Dany practically on the street. I've never done nearly that much PDA with Jesse, well, he hated it. It wasn't "proper." I shake away those thoughts.

We come to the elevators, getting on silently. I glance over at her as the doors shut, pulling out a pair of large, round sunglasses.

"You're not allergic to the sun, are you?" I ask tentatively.

"That's only vampires, honeybun."

"Oh, right...I knew that."

Seeing my reflection in the mirror, I smooth my hair a little and then my skirt again.

"You're perfect, Lucille."

Her comment stops me, and I blink up at her. I can't see her eyes, covered with those glasses. Yet, my stomach flips with a giddiness, I think.

How did I go down to the Underground, accidentally waiting for a mafia boss, only to be returning home with a goth stripper in 4-inch platforms who just said I'm perfect?

I'm half-tempted to pinch myself.

A wave of her perfume, scent I think it actually is, drifts over to me. It calms me, allowing those butterflies to settle into a comfortable warmth.

"Thank you." I stare down at the fibers of my sweater. I

purse my lips, trying to understand the kindness and sweetness from her, apart from fully believing she's attracted to me. Even if she truly is, and I know I am to her, that didn't mean she had to be this kind.

Dany's fingers lift my chin up, moving my gaze to see my reflection again. This time, I notice her beside me and us together—a tall goth succubus, next to a floral covered woman.

"Keep your eyes up, honeybun. They're too beautiful for the ground."

The doors open, and she lets go to lead us out onto the street. Keeping my head up, I stroll past her into the lingering rays of sun. Dany follows once more, slightly grumbling at the low sunlight, which almost makes me giggle as she adjusts her sunglasses.

From time to time, I notice people staring at Dany as we pass. She pays them no mind, looking very uninterested with everyone. We walk in amicable silence. I glance back at her, finding myself wanting those lips back on mine again.

The thought has me stumble over my own feet. I'm quickly caught by Dany, who grabs my arm and smirks at me. I blush, thanking her and we finally come upon my building's block.

"This is where you live?" I nod to her question, and she hums.

"You know this neighborhood?" I ask.

"Let's just say, it makes sense you heard about Alanzo from up here."

I stare at her a moment.

"It's a good choice," she adds.

A spark of pride hits me as we go into the building. "I found it on my own. My first place on my own."

She smiles as I lead her up the stairs, my steps somewhat slowing before we get to my floor. Breathing in deep, fortifying myself as we get to my hall, my heartrate eases as I unlock the door. Nothing seems tampered with.

I'm about to open the door, but Dany's hand covers mine on the handle.

"Let me check first, darling," she says calmly, and I step aside.

She steps in before me, eyes surveying the place as she investigates the small space. I tense up, wondering if I missed something, but more so if she'll be disappointed. My eyes flash to the laundry on my bed. The dishes still drying. The towel not folded.

Once more, I shake off those thoughts, reminding myself she's not Jesse and that it's *my* place. I breathe out slowly, trying to relax as I take solace in her care of checking the place. I drape my cardigan on a kitchen chair.

"Nothing appears tampered with," she says, stopping near the edge of my bed.

"This is your first time here," I say.

"And you've told me a lot about yourself." She takes her sunglasses off, smirking. "I know what clues to look for."

I hum. "And those are?"

"Maybe too much information for a first date. One of your neighbors is Riley, correct?"

"How'd you know that?" I step back, flicking my gaze to the door.

"Easy, honeybun." Calming perfume tickles my nose, helping me focus on the serenity on her face. The fog within my mind clearing more.

"You've planted yourself in the middle of a close-knit community," she explains. "I've known Riley for years, which means…" she saunters over to my refrigerator, somehow almost silent in those boots, and grabs a piece of paper from my notepad, "…him or you, call me in case whoever you're running from shows up."

She writes her number, and then I notice an address. I inhale sharply, taking it from her.

"And if you do want to talk to Alanzo, then I'll go with you."

"You would?"

She comes closer, cupping my cheek as she kisses my forehead. "Yes. Or if you ever want *me* to take care of them."

My eyes widen, heart beginning to thunder. I stare up at her. A piece of me wants her to hold me. Keep me safe in her arms.

"Don't disappear on me, honeybun," she whispers, words tender as she comes in close. "I'd hate to lose my precious light. With you I don't need sunglasses."

She kisses me softly. My breath stolen more from the sweet kiss.

Dany steps away, leaving me staring in disbelief as she leaves my apartment and closes the door. I touch my lips, burning for her. Just met or not, I've never felt this safe or more seen in my life.

CHAPTER 5
JESSE LOSES HIS TEMPER

I'M A BIGGER CHICKEN THAN THE ONES IN THE poultry section.

Four days since I've last seen Dany. Three days wondering if I should call her, especially after thinking Jesse was following me from work. Two days, since Rhonda walked me home, not knowing about Jesse, but agreed to anyway. And one day of me debating going back down to *Unbound* or not.

I've stress baked and cooked. Rhonda and my coworkers love me even more for all the treats I've brought. It calmed me, doing what I was passionate about, but it wasn't helping decide whether to contact a mafia boss about my problems or tell a succubus stripper I like her. A lot.

"Excuse me." A voice breaks me from my thoughts, and I blink up at a vampire.

"Oh, sorry," I say, stepping back from the meat counter.

They flash their fangs, smiling and give a wink. "No worries."

It's late in the evening. Most markets would be closing

soon, but this one was open until dawn. The vampire with low glowing red eyes and long hair steps past and grabs a couple of chicken cutlets. They nod at me and walk down the aisle.

I sigh, grabbing some cutlets for myself. Perhaps, I should just go down to *Unbound* again, and ask for help. But once again, I don't have the money to pay whatever services Alanzo may require to help me. And then I don't want Dany getting hurt trying to help me next.

A shiver runs down my spine, and I smooth my hand over my dress' bodice. Keeping my head up, ignoring the sinking feeling of despair that comes, I finish shopping. I leave the market, walking home lost in my thoughts.

Approaching my building, I look up and almost stumble when I see Jesse. My steps falter as I hurry up the steps, noticing him smoking and looking like a disheveled mess. I make it to the entrance, but it's too late.

"Lucy!" His voice echoes off the walls as I run.

My hands fumble for my keys. "Come on, come on."

The metal clatters against the door as I try to get the key into its slot. My bags feel too

heavy as my heart pounds within my chest. Damn it, why did he have to show up while Riley is at work. Who am I kidding, it's *why* he did. He doesn't stand a chance against a Paranormal being.

He huffs up the stairs, grumbling and thudding.

Finally, my door opens, and I scramble to get inside, but he grabs me. I'm yanked back, groceries spilling as he slams me against the wall.

"You really think you could leave me?" He spits into my face. Smokey breath invades my nostrils, making my stomach churn as I shove at him. He grabs at me as I slap at him, trying to get him off. "I am your *husband*!"

"Not anymore!" I scream, shoving harder. "Let me go!"

I bring my foot down, heel hitting his toes. He stumbles back enough for me to run into the apartment. I try to slam the door closed but he pushes in. I trip over myself, stumbling as I back away towards the kitchen. He spits onto my floor, grabbing at the few books I have and tosses them. He grabs a lamp, throwing it next and the bulb shatters. The apartment darkens as I continue to step back, chest heaving as my hands shake.

Jesse's eyes flare. His clothes are wrinkled and dirty. His hair mussed, and beard unkempt. He stalks towards me, pointing a finger at me.

"You're coming home with me, Lucy."

"No. I'm not," I state, bumping into the table.

"You've embarrassed me enough!"

"Leave, Jesse!"

"You're my wife!"

"We're not married anymore!" I argue, feeling behind me at the table. What did I leave out? What did I—

"Yes, we fucking are," he growls.

"Just because you refuse to sign the papers, doesn't mean we are. The judge ordered you to. I have a restraining order! You can't be here." I move around the table as he moves closer.

"Bullshit. You belong *to me*."

"No, I do *not*."

"Lucy, I'm ordering—"

Rage builds up within me. "Fuck you!"

I grab a pan I laid out, swinging it just as he lunges. He yells when I hit him across the face, and I swing again. He falls against the wall, howling as I drop the pan and it clatters to the ground.

I sprint around the table, running for the hall. He groans behind me as I slam the door, locking it behind me in hopes of slowing him. My feet scream as I race down the steps and out into the evening crowds. I don't look back as I run, losing speed as I aim for the Main Entrance, until I hear him behind me. I'm slowing quickly, not fast enough to outrun him.

Almost frantic, I see a bar up ahead with plenty of werewolves outside. Glancing over my shoulder, I see Jesse storming for me and pushing people away. I duck into the bar, looking behind me again, but run right into someone.

"I'm sorry, I just—"

"Whoa, hey, you okay?" A large grey werewolf grabs my arms to steady me. He's wearing a…kilt? Just that. A kilt. "I get really needing a drink."

"No, my ex…" my voice softens, looking over my shoulder, "…my ex he…"

"Don't need to tell me twice." The werewolf slides an arm over my shoulders, turning us away from the door and moving further into the bar.

The floor is somewhat sticky and televisions play loudly. It smells of beer and cherries, everything is lit up by LED lights of several colors. It's hazy from smoke. The werewolf guides me to a booth, letting me sit and hide from the door's view. Green eyes shimmer down at me as he smiles.

"Good and tucked away. Name's Zane, by the way." He holds a large hand out.

"Lucille." I shake it, and mine feels like a child's within his.

"Well, can't let your night go to waste. Want a drink?" He glances over his shoulder, and the lights catch his grey skin and fur around his shoulders oddly.

"No, thank you," I say, peeking around him and see Jesse through the glass door. I duck back, heart pounding. "Actually, can I borrow a phone?"

———

The bar door slams open, and there's a sweep of a spicy scent across the bar.

I jolt even next to Zane, who I think could throw a truck. Zane doesn't seem fazed, and chuckles when he sees who it is.

It's Dany.

Her eyes search the place, landing on me finally. The intensity on her face doesn't ease as she prowls past customers, who practically part like the seas for her. She's in even taller platform boots, wearing a skirt that has slits up to her hip, along with a corset that barely contains her breasts, and a dark, floor length jacket with spikes on the shoulders.

"So, that's who you called," Zane chuckles.

"You know Dany?" I watch her approach like an angry hurricane. Maybe I should've waited until she got here to explain everything. She seemed calm on the phone, but I'm realizing it was quiet wrath.

"Yeah, she's cool. Not just cause of her aesthetic, but she's fun," Zane answers, grinning. I'm worried about his idea of fun. "What up, Dany Stormborn?"

She ignores him, zeroing in on me as she towers over me in my seat. I give a tentative smile. Although she's scary at the moment, all I feel is relief.

Dany leans down. "Did he harm you?"

My brows pinch, knowing I told her everything on the phone. "I told—"

"I mean, Balto over here."

"Hey, wrong nickname," Zane grumbles playfully. "It's Pongo."

"No, no," I quickly say. "He's been very nice. A real gentleman...gentle-wolf."

Her furious blue eyes calm, looking me over. Emotions tumble, surprise most of all that she cared that much. I knew she'd come, and liked me, but this was...something more.

"Are you hurt?" Her voice gentles, cupping my cheek.

"I'm alright. Maybe some bruises later, nothing makeup can't cover."

Dany's eyes harden again, and practically growls under her breath as she straightens and lets go of me. She and Zane exchange a look. "Thank you for watching her."

He shrugs, unperturbed by her intense aura, but his eyes do shift warily over me. Was it something I said?

"Well, don't want word getting to baby sis and her Pops I'm not helpful," he smirks. Dany flicks a look to me.

"Wait, baby sis? Who is that, I've heard that name before," I ask.

"Someone scarier than Dany," Zane muses.

Dany's expression relaxes again, giving him a bored look. "Who do you think taught her? The vampires?"

Zane chuckles, and I'm definitely confused. I'm certainly missing something.

"Come on, honeybun, let's get you home before the wolves want to play fetch," Dany says, and I gasp at her remark.

"Dany—"

Zane grins, winks, and waves off the remark. Dany takes my hand, leading me out of the booth in my confused state.

"Thank you, Zane, it was a pleasure meeting you," I say, and he tips his head.

Dany places me before her, beginning to guide me out of the bar.

"Want help finding the fucker?" Zane asks.

"As if I've ever needed a male's help," Dany responds.

The crowd splits again, easily allowing us through as we

come out into the very late night. It's the middle of the day for Dany and other Paranormals, who've crowded the walks. I pause outside the bar, searching the crowd as I smooth my hands down my skirt.

Dany places her hand against the small of my back. "You're safe with me, honeybun."

I tilt my head back. She looms over me, placing me under her shadow. Her blue eyes warm and glowing as she leans down and briefly places a tender kiss upon my lips. My breath catches, swallowing hard after she stands tall again. She gently encourages me to walk, and we weave through the crowd.

"So, it's your ex-husband you're running from," she says.

"Yes. Although he doesn't believe he is."

"He soon will."

I look up at her, finding those lines of fury gone. There's calmness, which I don't understand. She doesn't seem at all worried about Jesse. Then again, she hasn't fought him off today or beat him with a pan.

"How are you not scared?"

"I haven't survived the horrors of mankind to allow an insignificant man to scare me now."

My heart thunders, remembering her age. What has she seen? Survived?

"How'd you move on?"

"Who said I truly have?"

My hand finds hers, gripping it and she squeezes mine. We come to my building and my stomach clenches. She leads the way to my door, where the groceries still lay in a mess with the door open. Dany helps me clean, putting away the surviving groceries, and then checks my apartment for anything else Jesse may have left.

He only left his mess behind. As always.

"Thank you for coming back with me," I say, glancing

over at my dented pan. "I'd offer you something to eat, but it'll take a moment to make anything since he destroyed most of my groceries. Although, I have some carrot cake left over from the office."

She quirks a brow. "Quite the cook. My talents aren't for the kitchen."

"Usually, it calms me. It was my happier moments, tonight though…" my voice trails away, as I sigh, "…I'm not so sure."

"Could offer me something else to eat."

It takes a moment before my eyes snap to hers, widening.

"Just thought you'd might like a distraction," she muses, taking her jacket off and putting it over my armchair. "No pressure, honeybun, just an idea. We can also stay in and read."

That sultry look is upon her face. Her perfume strengthens, and I breathe deeply of its scent. It drifts around me, helping me forget who stormed into my kitchen.

"I can smell you," I suddenly state, and her brows lift. "Like this flowery, spicey perfume that helps me breathe. Think. Sometimes confusing, but are you doing that on purpose?"

Dany saunters towards me, once more far too silent in those boots of hers. I'm barely to her chest as she gazes down at me, leaning closer.

"Honeybun, I've only used a fraction of my powers and it was in *Unbound*. Part of the job to keep customers happy and calm. Not ever since."

"At all?"

She shakes her head.

So, I was sensing…*her*.

"Remember what I said, darling?" She asks. "Attraction is attraction. So, is that what you desire? Me?"

My heart beats too fast, butterflies coming back. Desire does pull at me, yearning for her to kiss and hold me. I inhale sharply, shuddering at how much I do want her. So very much after today, to feel what I felt in that club again.

In a faint voice, mustering up my courage, I offer quietly, "Would you like something else to eat?"

CHAPTER 6
LUCILLE LEARNS TO SCISSOR

An alluring smile grows on her. "I'd love that."

Her lips press against mine delicately. I lean into her and allow myself to skim my tongue over hers. She does the gesture back, elation flicking through me. Dany suddenly grips my hips, hauling me up against her body. I gasp, flinging my arms around her shoulders as I go back to kissing her with a moan. A purring sound comes from Dany, causing a shiver to run over my skin as she easily carries me over to a wall, pressing my back against it. She pins me with her body, hands sliding up under my skirt to tease the seam of my underwear. I break the kiss with a gasp.

Soft lips caress my neck, moving down to my chest. Her slick tongue slides just at the crevice of my breasts. Pleasure courses through me and I feel drunk with her touch.

Dany leans back, smiling as she runs her tongue over the top of her teeth. She caresses my cheek, then strokes her fingers into my hair with tender care.

"Oh, you are gorgeous."

"So are you," I whisper, staring into glowing cobalt eyes.

They glow brighter as she pulls me away from the wall, putting me onto the bed. "Certain about this, honeybun?"

I nod eagerly, anticipation rising at the new experience and just wanting Dany to never stop. She smirks, sliding her hands back up my thighs to their apex. Fingers trace over the thin fabric of my underwear. A grin comes over her as she gets onto her knees.

"Why are—oh!" Dany dives under my skirt, kissing directly onto my sex. Warmth cascades over my skin, panties becoming soaked. I reach down, trying to find her under my skirt, but quickly give up and grab the comforter.

Dany tugs down my panties, causing me to lift my hips as she drags them down my legs. She kisses up the inside of my thighs, trailing towards her destination. My breathing picks up, heart frantic as a singular long lick is given through my center. She continues to eat me out in a way I've never thought possible. Her tongue and mouth pressed against me with a fervent hunger. My thighs are gripped, held open for her as she feasts on me below. Tugging at the blankets, my body shakes as my hips want to press closer to the pierced tongue that flicks over my clit.

"Oh…Dany!" I scream.

She sucks harder and my mind goes black. My body goes taut as she keeps pace as pleasure washes over me. Sparks fly up my spine, zapping from where she licks. Finally, she presses the flat of her tongue against me as I feel myself come down from the high, going limp.

Dany comes out from her tent, grinning mischievously as she licks away the moisture around her lips and chin.

"I'm a messy eater, but don't worry, I'm excellent at cleaning up," she states, tilting her head at me. "Desire more, honeybun?"

Without a thought, enraptured by the goth succubus and wanting more, I answer, "Yes, please."

She hums, beginning to unzip the front of her corset. "Such good manners. Clothes off, sweetheart."

In my post-bliss state, I pull off my clothes as Dany does. Laying naked on my bed, she stands fully nude before me. Her nipples are pierced, matching the others with black metallic. Just when I think she couldn't be more beautiful her wings appear. They don't thrust out from nothing, but shimmer into existence behind her. The leathery wings a darker shade of her skin.

I gasp, "How?"

They flutter slightly as she crawls onto the bed towards me. "Magic."

I giggle at the teasing in her voice, while she climbs on top of me and kisses my neck.

"Touch me, honeybun."

Her scent consumes me as I tentatively reach up to stroke her skin. I become bolder as I move to squeeze her breasts. She moans, licking my nipple in response. We continue to feel each other, caressing and teasing. I take the time I've never had before to explore another body, flushed against mine as her lips trail along my skin.

Suddenly, she sits up, smiling with glee. She starts to resituate my body and hers, wrapping our legs around the other. She partially sits up, pulling me up as well with one of our legs behind the other. She's between my legs, and I'm between hers. Dany then presses her sex against mine, rolling her hips lightly. Grabbing my hands, she puts them upon her breasts as she grinds her pelvis into mine.

I gasp at the new sensation, gripping her chest as I grind back. Suddenly, I feel a vibration from her. It pulsates, thrumming almost as I gasp with surprise. Thrusting her hips forward, she presses her sex against mine and the vibrations become stronger, going straight to my core.

"Dany…is your…oh, fuck!" I'm cut off by a gasping moan as her finger teases my clit.

"Succubi and incubi are built for essentially two things, darling: pleasure and pain." Her wings splay out behind her fluttering as her head rolls back.

The strong pulsations from her sex makes my legs shake, tightening around her as I grip her arms next. My body catapults towards ecstasy, faster and stronger than I've ever known. Dany continues to roll and gyrate her hips, rubbing against my center as she fingers me. I grasp her thigh, nails digging into her skin as she groans with pleasure. Bliss fogs my mind, hearing, seeing, and feeling only Dany around me.

Body shaking, my head is thrown back as I scream quietly as Dany moans. Going taut once more, I come as she does. The vibrations stop as we both go limp, falling over onto my bed. Our legs are still tangled around the other as she pulls me against her body.

"I didn't know succubi could vibrate their vaginas?"

She chuckles against my ear, kissing my jaw. "Also *ribbed* for pleasure."

Relaxed and sated, I giggle as I snuggle closer to her while she strokes my hair, falling asleep in the comfort of her arms. Safe and content.

CHAPTER 7
LUCILLE KNOWS JESSE IS TRYING TO MURDER HER

POUNDING WAKES ME; RATTLING THE WALLS. I SIT up, grasping for the bed covers as the door slams open. A scream releases from my throat as Jesse breaks in, pointing a gun towards me.

"If I can't have—"

"Oh, shut up." Dany's voice cuts through the air.

My eyes snap to her, noticing she's lounging against the wall next to me. The blanket doesn't cover her chest, revealing her ample breasts. Jesse finally sees her and starts to point the gun at her. His face torn between disgust and arousal.

"Who the fuck are you, bi—"

"I said…*Shut. Up.*" Her voice pierces once more, but this time Jesse shuts his mouth. He points the gun back at me, but his hand begins to tremble. "Drop the gun."

The gun clatters to the floor.

I stare, gaping in shock as Dany slowly steps from the bed, fully nude. She walks over to him, then whispers something into his ear. He falls to his knees, slamming hard to the wood floor. Something thumps against it. I lean up, clutching the blanket as I see his head pressed against the wood. Dany shuts the door, locking it.

Jesse doesn't move.

"Dany...what's happening?"

"Two purposes, honeybun," she answers in a calm tone. She stops beside him, eyes glowing with fury. Her wings shudder, rising up and scraping against the ceiling.

"What?"

"Pleasure and..." her gaze meets mine, the perfume I know billowing through the apartment, but with a foreboding wrongness to it, "...pain."

Suddenly, I can't smell it, but I can somehow feel it in the room.

Carefully, I step out of bed, keeping the blanket around me. I stare at my ex-husband on the floor, kneeling with his head shoved against the ground, hands fisted and shaking. I look back at Dany.

"I won't hurt you," she says gently.

"I hope so, given I'd like to do what we did again." My eyes go wide, as she smirks. "I don't know why I said that." My grip tightens as she walks over, stroking a hand over my hair. The glowing of her eyes is different than earlier this evening. "What are you doing to him?"

"I'm one of the few succubi who can manipulate fear easily, but only to singular individuals. Mainly because I know how to couple it with desire, such as..." she gives him a disdainful look, then speaks in a voice that's almost not hers, "...beg, little boy. Beg me."

Jesse mumbles against the wood, blubbering things I can't decipher.

"Plead for my love. Simper and whine."

Her voice is hypnotic as Jesse starts doing vulgar things with his body, thrusting himself against the flood. He continues to mumble, laying on the floor as he begs and whines for her to use him. Fuck him. Love him. Put him out of his misery.

I stare at the scene before me. This has to be a dream.

So easily she has full control of him. Again, I remember how old she is.

"What do you want, Lucille?" She strokes the side of my face, eyes soft only for me. Yet, rage lines the edges of her face.

I swallow hard. Mind frantic with thoughts as suddenly I'm not the one without control, but with all of it.

Jesse whimpers louder, banging his hands against the floor for Dany's attention. She snaps her gaze to him. *"Crawl to the corner, naughty boy."*

He does, giving desperate sounds as he pushes himself into the corner of the kitchen. A memory flashes in my mind from years ago of myself cowering in fear of him killing me.

"My kind can easily manipulate cravings and fears, twisting them if we must for advantages," she explains, cupping my cheek to focus on her. "I've learned to combine both, like many succubi, but a bit stronger than some. I've had good teachers. So...what do you want done with him, darling?"

My heart pounds in my chest as I glimpse over at Jesse. I've feared him for so long, it's odd being in the same room and not feel terrified. My face goes pale as it starts to sink in, he broke into my apartment to kill me. And Dany.

Dany's wings move down, cocooning me from the room, just her and I.

"I never want to see him again," I whisper. "I want to stop running."

"Then no one shall ever see him again. Ever."

"I don't give a fuck about him, but I don't want you in trouble." I clutch at her arms. "Or owe your boss. I don't—"

She gently hushes me, kissing my cheek. "Oh, darling I don't need permission to take out the trash."

"But...what..."

She cups my face, and her scent drifts under my nose, calming me. I breathe deep as she silently soothes me.

"I've spent *decades* hunting cruel beings like him. If you wish, I'll wield the knife for you."

She caresses my chin, thumb stroking under my lip. Morals fight inside me. I should just send him to the authorities. Except, they've been no help. I've been on my own, losing ground slowly as Jesse's stalked and practically hunted me. Tears gather, some falling. Dany catches them with a delicate grace.

"Let your rage speak for you, Lucille," she says, holding my chin up.

My chin quivers, standing straighter. I want to be free. I want to be happy and not always looking over my shoulder. Images of the bruises he's given me, the pain, the defeat, and loss. Finally, the rage.

Shakingly, inhaling sharply, I say, "I want him gone. Forever."

Dany kisses my forehead. "Cover your eyes if you must."

She turns, wings moving away as she glares over at Jesse.

"*Crawl*," she orders. He does as she walks around him, stopping him. A finger traces over his jaw to the top of his head, and it takes a moment for me to realize she's scratched him as blood forms.

"I abhor men like you," she states, stepping into the kitchen and coming back with a butcher's knife. "Thinking you own a woman; own any female because of your twisted, self-righteous, superiority that doesn't exist. All because you can't admit you are inferior, yet you fake incompetence and values to cover your insidious thoughts."

She grabs his hair, pulling his head back. His eyelids

droop, moaning as she places the knife against his neck. He babbles more nonsense, licking his lips and thrusting his hips in the air like a lovesick pervert.

"What's worse is that I'm not even making you desire anything that's not already in your filthy head," she growls as he starts to scratch at his groin. "It's just out in the open for all to see."

I gasp, stepping back in horror.

"Take the knife, hold it to your throat, pitiful creature," she orders, and he does. She stands behind him, foreboding as her wings flare out. "Any last words you want from him? Even if they're torn from his throat?"

I stare at my ex-husband, whom I designed my entire life around only to be betrayed, abused, and hunted. Treated as a thing and made to feel like nothing. The man I hoped would have a semblance of kindness, but that last string of hope is cut as I glance at the gun he aimed. Anger grips me.

"No," I say.

There's a punch to the air, the tainted perfume comes back like a vice grip around my throat. I cover my mouth and nose, stepping back again as Dany stands taller with a vengeful aura. She places a hand over his head, gripping him harshly as pricks of blood form where her nails are.

"Beg."

Jesse mutters words, tears falling down his face as he sputters.

"Close your eyes, Lucille."

I do.

There's movement before I hear something squish and then a crunch. There's more stabbing sounds, and I flinch as gurgling follows. I listen as Jesse plunges the large knife into killing himself on my kitchen floor. There's finally a heavy wet thud and clatter. I open one eye, seeing him slumped in a mess. Blood pools around him with the knife beside his limp body.

I stare at the dead man.

Dany leans down, grabs the knife, and plunges it into his chest.

My mind goes blank. The next moment Dany stands in front of me and cups my face with her hands. I meet her eyes.

"Your eyes are too beautiful for that filth."

I dive into her embrace, shuddering as she wraps her arms and wings around me. I cry silently in relief against her skin, feeling as if I can fully breathe for the first time in over a decade.

CHAPTER 8
AND DANY, LOVES ME

THE AIR IS THICK WITH PHEROMONES. I HUM AT the soothing smell and feel, crossing my ankles as I sit at the bar of *Unbound*. I'm on my second Sweet Paradise cocktail, glancing over at Bobby who gives me a wink. I check myself in the mirror behind the bar, smiling softly at my curls and then smooth my hands down my soft pink dress, covered in daises. It has sleeves down to the elbow. I adore it for the lace at its sleeves and along the bust.

A song finishes, and I look up as a couple of strippers leave the stage with a flourish, including Dany. I smile as her eyes point in my direction, and a sultry smile comes over her face. She disappears into the shadows.

It's been two weeks since Jesse was forever removed from my life.

I've been staying with Dany until my apartment is thoroughly cleaned. It has been six days, but I like her kitchen more anyway.

Women cheer for the next stripper that comes on stage, which is an incubus. I sigh at the sense of safety and enjoyment here. I've grown used to it, finding it a haven not just because of Dany, but the entire club. So much so, that I've forgotten who owns it.

Until now.

"Evening, boss," Bobby greets.

I give him a confused look as he grabs some glasses, and then I notice an incubus standing behind me in the mirror.

I spin in my seat as he smiles warmly. His violet eyes are gentle as he holds his hand out for me to shake. "You must be Lucille."

"I am. Pleasure to meet you." I shake his hand briefly.

"I've been told you waited for me a few weeks back. My apologies you waited so long, only to meet now."

My brows raise. "Meet?"

"I'm Alanzo Cuorebella. Owner of *Unbound*."

Slowly, my face falls as I recognize him as the incubus I ran from weeks ago. Thoughts whirl as I realize a mafia boss is standing in front of me.

"Dany told me everything," he says as I stare at him. "I wanted to introduce myself properly, meet the woman who's captured her heart. And to inform you everything has been taken care of." He leans in closer, smelling of cigars and cinnamon. "His death was ruled as a suicide."

"Oh," I blink, coming out of my stupor. "Oh, thank you. If you want payment, I could try—"

He shakes his head. "My hope in this life is to help those who need it, especially those who've fought for their freedom. You're safe and welcome here whenever you need, Lucille, whether Dany is working or not. If you ever require help, just ask."

I nod, speechless at his candor and gentleness. Is he actually a mafia boss? He seems too kind.

"If and when you're ready, I'd be delighted for you to meet my Mate. You two have similar tastes." Alanzo smiles as I glance down at my outfit, confused as he starts to walk away, but pauses. "Oh, and Riley told me you're the one who moved into my baby girl's old apartment."

"Your ba—...the librarian is your daughter?"

"Yes. Hope the shelves I built are to your liking." He smirks, walking away.

I stare, unsure of what just happened. I'm *living* in a mafia boss' daughter's old apartment. The mafia boss I accidentally tried to meet on my own.

"Okay there, Lucille?" Bobby asks, coming around.

"Just realizing how odd life is."

"Tell me about it," he chuckles. "Learn just to lean into it. Hey, Dany."

Dany approaches, wearing her signature platform boots, lacing up past her knee. She's changed into a latex dress which clings to her body. Chains of various sizes hang from her neck, clipped onto bands on her arms down to her forearms. She smirks, stopping in front of me before kissing me deeply. I hum, tingling with desire as I grab her hand, tongues dancing around the other. Her perfume is far more enticing than the club could ever be.

"Hello, honeybun," she greets against my lips, then kisses my neck. "Enjoy the show?"

"Yes, and you were wonderful. Although, I may never understand how you're able to do some of those moves in those boots."

"Practice, sweetheart. As you've learned the last few days." She nibbles my ear.

Holding back laughter, I place a hand on her shoulder to ease her back. I raise a brow. "Did you know who owned my apartment before I did?"

"Yeah, baby sis did."

I lightly smack her arm, trying to seem frustrated, but a smile pulls at my lips instead as she smirks. "You didn't tell me? Is this the same baby sis Zane and you mentioned?"

"There's only one baby sis of the Underground. Didn't seem important at the time."

I give her a bored expression. "Dany."

She lifts my chin with a finger. "You were unsure and scared; it wasn't going to help at the time. Or be a good first date topic."

"Uh-huh."

She holds her hand out, helping me down from my seat. As always, she towers over me, leading me out of the club.

"Should I be worried that I moved into an apartment once owned by a mafia boss' daughter?"

"Technically, he isn't anymore."

I stop, pulling my hand from her grasp and folding my arms as I give her a raised brow. "What?"

Her face is passive, looking down at me from her height. She comes in close, stroking her fingers through my hair.

"He was for over a century," she says. "Only recently has he handed his position to his eldest son, but he's still very much involved. To me, he's still the boss. Like for many. I told you an outdated truth, but…I apologize."

"Why didn't you tell me that?"

"You were desperate. Too many times I've seen desperate beings make rash decisions. I trust Alanzo, but you'd have never told me the truth either if I had."

I sigh. She stands up straight, waiting for me as the next song plays and the stage lights shift. Without a lick of guilt on her face, she says, "And I was selfish of you."

She isn't perfect, and a bit passionate, but as I stare up at the succubus who killed my abusive ex…I can't be mad at her. Well, I don't *want* to be mad at her. I hold my hand out, "No more outdated truths."

She takes it, the corner of her mouth going up. "Yes, my perfect storm."

We leave *Unbound*, nodding at Darius as we go out into

the glistening Underground as the lights above twinkle. Dany stays beside me, always my protective shadow as we stroll over the brick paths towards her place.

"Besides..." she breaks the quiet, "...perhaps you won't be living in that apartment much longer to have to worry about it."

I almost stumble and stop, looking up to find blue eyes glittering against her dark eye shadow. Unconsciously, I squeeze her hand. "Are you asking...me to move in with you?"

"Yes, when you're ready."

"How? I'm human."

"You can move down here if your partner is Paranormal and vouches for you. Besides my boss is in the mafia, I think you'll be fine moving down here. Unless you prefer Topside."

"My job?"

"I'll walk you every day."

I laugh, covering her hand with my other hand. "Dany."

She leans in close, kissing my cheek. "I'm certain I fell for you the moment you walked into *Unbound*, honeybun." Blue eyes glow warmly. "I already love you, sweetheart. Are you open to loving me in return?"

Her voice is tender, more than it ever has been. Smiling, I reach up and cup her face, happiness filling me. "I'm certain I already love you, too."

I tug her towards me for a kiss. Soft lips caress mine, elation sparking over me as desire soon follows. Her hands slip to the nape of my neck, holding me as we fervently kiss. My hands run down to her neck, trailing fingers over the chains that dangle.

"Let's go home," she murmurs against my lips.

"I'll bake your favorite." Her eyes go alight as we step

apart, holding hands to stroll together. "Lemon meringue pie."

"Oh, we both know my favorite is a honey bun." Dany teasingly traces her tongue over her teeth, flashing her piercing. "After such a long night at work, I'm ravenous."

I laugh at her, feeling that sense of freedom wash over me along with love. The Underground, my likely new home, surrounds us in noise and pulsating lights. Smiles break out on both our faces, gripping each other's hand warmly. Just a goth stripper and ex-housewife on their way home for some dessert.

WANT MORE OF THE UNDERGROUND?

Need more than just this taste of the Underground of New York City?
Need to know who used to own the apartment before Lucille?
Get to know more about Alanzo Courebella?
You can read all about them in the first book of the "Mafia, Murder, and Mayhem Series"

"Vinny the Vampire & Me"

BOOKS BY ELM JED

Mafia, Murder, and Mayhem Series
Vinny the Vampire & Me
Sweet Cheeks & Her Mob Boss
The Wolf Boss & His Darling
The Werecat & Her Lone Wolf: A Novella
Memories of the Underground: Volume One

Contemporary Mafia Series
My Dear Watson
My Forgotten Demons
My Emerald Fire
My Dear Leo

ABOUT THE AUTHOR

Elm Jed is a Marine Corps veteran, who's been writing since they were ten years old with a degree in Theatre. They live with their husband, who is their biggest supporter from making sure they're caffeinated to listening to them ramble for hours about chaotic ideas. They spend most of their time jotting down ideas, reading novellas that make them laugh, or attending Renaissance Festivals with their greatest friends.

www.ingramcontent.com/pod-product-compliance
Lightning Source LLC
Chambersburg PA
CBHW022049170626
46808CB00003B/1417